DIARY OF AN
ICE PRINCESS

The Big Freeze

For Ryder and Hunter

Copyright © 2020 by Christina Soontornvat

Illustrations by Barbara Szepesi Szucs copyright © 2020 by Scholastic Inc.

All rights reserved. Published by Scholastic Inc., *Publishers since 1920.* SCHOLASTIC and associated logos are trademarks and/or registered trademarks of Scholastic Inc.

ISBN 978-1-338-35401-0

10 9 8 7 6 5 4 3 2   20 21 22 23 24

Printed in the U.S.A. 23

First printing 2020

Book design by Yaffa Jaskoll

DIARY OF AN ICE PRINCESS

The Big Freeze

by
Christina Soontornvat

Illustrations by
Barbara Szepesi Szucs

SCHOLASTIC INC.

The Art of Surprise

☀ FRIDAY ☀

Dear Diary,

I've said this before, but I'll say it again: There is nothing I love more than school.

Except my family.

And my dog, Gusty.

Okay, and maybe my best friend, Claudia.

Okay, and maybe mango-and-whipped-cloud pudding–but you get the picture!

If the kids at school knew about my real life–that I'm a princess with magical winter powers who lives in a palace in the clouds—they'd probably wish we could trade places. But I just love knowing that when I walk through the doors of Hilltop Science and Arts Academy something exciting is going to happen.

Exciting things that could happen:

❋ Sharpening pencils!

❋ Holding doors open for people!

❋ Drinking milk out of a carton!

❋ Riding on an actual school bus!

Of course the best thing about school is science class. Our teacher, Ms. Collier, comes up with the coolest experiments. Which is why I was so happy this morning to hear her say, "Class, I have a very exciting project to tell you about!"

What would it be? Sharks? Electricity? How sharks use electricity to catch prey?

Nope. It turns out she was talking about *art*.

"Class, this week we will begin working on our biggest art project of the year."

Okay, that sounded fine. Maybe I'd draw a diagram of sharks, or electricity . . .

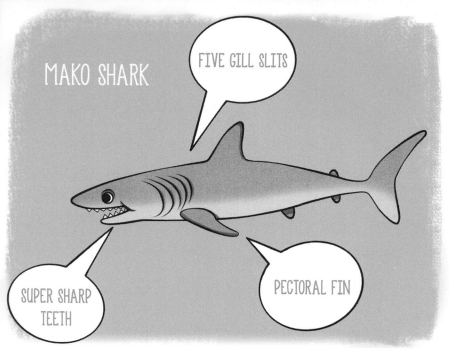

Ms. Collier continued, "The project is called *This Is Me*, and it should be an artistic expression of what makes *you* special. I'm giving you a lot of freedom with this project. You can do just about anything you want."

"Anything?" I squeaked.

"Anything." She smiled. "You can use any materials you find at home, or you can even do a performance. Just make sure your artwork will fit through the door because all projects will be shared at the Family Showcase."

There went my idea for a life-size cardboard model of a mako shark.

"My only other rule," said Ms. Collier, "is that you do this project on your own. No help from friends or family, please."

My best friend, Claudia, leaned in close. "I love projects with hardly any rules. This is going to be so much fun!"

There is a saying that goes,

"Opposites attract." That is true for
magnets and best friends. While Claudia
was excited about the art project,
the whole thing was giving me the cold
sweats!

2

The Royal We

Whenever you see a royal family in the movies, it always seems like they have such easy lives. They sip tea, go to parties, and glide around in big, poofy dresses.

In *my* family, being royalty means

doing work. Everyone in our family has
a very important job. (Okay, everyone
except Gusty. His only job is getting ear
scratches.)

For example, my mom and
grandfather are both Windtamers, which
means they can control the wind and
weather. Mom's job is to bring the spring

rains. Granddad is the North Wind. I love him so much, but sometimes—

"LINA, MY FAVORITE GRANDDAUGHTER FINALLY DECIDED TO SHOW UP!"

—his big, booming voice can get a little intense.

I go to Granddad's castle every Saturday to practice my magic. I'm a Winterheart, which means my powers are all about ice and snow.

"So what are we doing today, Granddad?" I asked him this morning. "Sleet-making? Icicle-shaping? A little polar vortex formation?"

"LINA, TODAY I WANT TO TALK ABOUT *THE CHOOSING.*"

"Oh, okay. Well, I really like those sesame crackers you buy, so–"

"I DON'T MEAN CHOOSING SNACKS! I MEAN CHOOSING YOUR PATH IN LIFE. WE HAVE BEEN PRACTICING MANY DIFFERENT KINDS OF WINTER

Granddad doesn't pass out a lot of
compliments, so I was very proud to
hear him say that. When I first started
my lessons with him, I couldn't keep my
winter magic under control at all. But
now I've learned so much.

"WHEN YOU GROW UP, YOU WILL HAVE A VERY IMPORTANT TASK, JUST LIKE YOUR MOTHER AND ME. YOU ARE DOING SO WELL WITH YOUR WINTER MAGIC THAT I THINK YOU COULD BE READY TO CHOOSE YOUR TASK VERY SOON."

"Seriously?" I gulped. "Doesn't that seem early?"

"THE SOONER YOU CHOOSE YOUR TASK, THE SOONER YOU CAN BEGIN FOCUSING YOUR SKILLS, WHICH ARE GETTING STRONGER EVERY DAY."

Gosh, Diary, Granddad had never praised my skills so much before. I felt like I couldn't say no.

But choosing the job I'm going to have for the rest of my life? That's a much bigger decision than picking out an afternoon snack!

3

The Cold Shoulder

We have two weeks to work on our *This Is Me* project, but I wanted to get an early start.

Last night I grew two batches of crystals using different salts. I measured them, recorded the results, and dyed them turquoise (they just look more crystal-ish when they are that color). I made a poster of the whole experiment and brought it to school to show Ms. Collier.

I thought she would be excited to see my art project, but instead she just looked confused.

"Lina, this is wonderful, but it seems more like a science experiment than an art project," she said.

"Even though I dyed the crystals turquoise?"

"Art is more than just adding color to something," said Ms. Collier. "This project should be an expression of what makes you special."

I started to tell her that growing crystals under my bed was one thing that made me special, but I knew she wouldn't go for it. She was right. A science experiment was not going to work for my art project. But I was still clueless about what *would* work.

I sighed. "To tell you the truth, Ms. Collier, I wish this project had a few more rules."

She smiled. "Making art sometimes involves a lot of starting over. You'll figure this out, Lina. Try to loosen up and have fun with it."

Fun? I could do that. And I knew just where to start.

Claudia and her family are the only ones who know all about my real life. Her house is the only place on the ground where I'm allowed to do my winter magic. Luckily, that's exactly where I was headed after school.

After we played for a while, Claudia showed me her art project. Diary, it was really cool! She's making a collage, which is a piece of art created from lots of different things.

"Wow," I said, looking closer. "I love how you made this out of stuff from your real life. That's such a great idea."

"Thanks! My mom got pretty mad when I glued her earring to it, but otherwise I'm happy with it. How's your project coming?"

"Oh you know, it's great . . ."

"Hold on. You haven't started working on it yet, have you?"

(Diary, Claudia supposedly has no magic, but I swear she has the power to read my mind.)

"I *have been* working on it, but I have to start over. Ms. Collier says

I can't do a science experiment. I have

zero idea what to do."

Claudia placed the back of her hand

on my forehead.

"What are you doing?" I asked.

"I'm taking your artistic temperature,"

she said. "So we can figure out what sort of project will fit you best."

"What are you—the art doctor?"

Claudia smiled. "Yup. And lucky for you, the doctor is *in*."

4

The Doctor Will See You Now

Diary, the art doctor had a lot of prescriptions for me.

First we painted.

"Lina, that's a beautiful chicken!" said Claudia.

"Ugh. It's supposed to be my dog."

"Oh. How about we try chalk pastels?"

We chalked.

"Is it a pirate ship?" Claudia asked.

"Ugh. It's supposed to be a castle!"

"Oh. How about we try clay?"

We sculpted.

Claudia looked nervous about guessing what my sculpture was.

"Mushrooms?" she said. "No, I've got it. Meerkats!"

I flopped down onto the floor and sighed. "It's supposed to be a sculpture of my *family*. Ugh, this is useless! I'm just not artistic."

"That's not true," said Claudia. "You're

one of the most creative people I know."

"Then why do the things I create look nothing like they're supposed to?" I groaned.

"I think you're too worried about making it look perfect," said Claudia. "Your project can look like anything as long as it shows something about who you are."

"But how can I do that? I'm not allowed to do science. I'm not allowed to use my powers. I can't reveal anything about my castle or my magic. What else can I do to show who I am?"

Claudia tapped her chin, but even the art doctor was stumped.

"I don't know," she said finally. "But whatever you do, you need to start working on it or you're going to run out of time."

Sadly, Diary, I didn't need an art doctor to give me that diagnosis.

5

The Book of Skies

✳ SATURDAY ✳

Unlike school, where I'm not allowed
to use my winter magic at all, at
Granddad's castle winter magic is the
only thing on the agenda.

"LINA, HAVE YOU BEEN THINKING

ABOUT WHICH TASK YOU WILL
CHOOSE?'"

"I have been thinking, but I'm
not sure yet. It's such an important
decision."

"I HAVE AN IDEA THAT MAY
HELP. COME. I HAVE SOMETHING TO
SHOW YOU.'"

I followed Granddad to his castle
library. He took down a gigantic, old-
looking book and set it on a table.

"THIS BOOK HAS A RECORD OF EVERY MEMBER OF OUR FAMILY AND THEIR CHOSEN TASK. SOON YOU WILL WRITE YOUR OWN NAME IN THIS BOOK AND THE TASK OF YOUR CHOOSING."

Wow, Diary. I felt a tingling all the way from my fingertips to my ears. This book was really special.

Granddad flipped the old, crumbly pages until he got to a section titled "Winterhearts." It showed all the members of our family who had winter magic—just like me. Next to their names was a description of their Tasks.

"READING WHAT OTHER WINTERHEARTS HAVE DONE BEFORE

YOU MAY HELP YOU DECIDE WHAT
TO DO."

While Granddad told old stories about
the Winterhearts who came before me,
I started to read down the list.

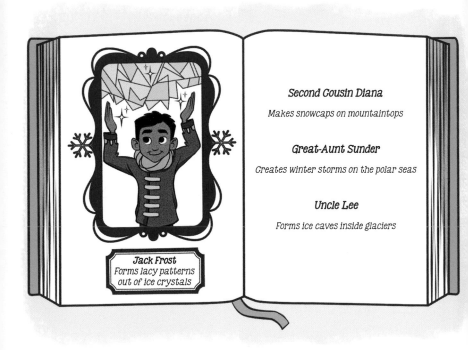

Second Cousin Diana
Makes snowcaps on mountaintops

Great-Aunt Sunder
Creates winter storms on the polar seas

Uncle Lee
Forms ice caves inside glaciers

Jack Frost
*Forms lacy patterns
out of ice crystals*

"WELL, LINA? WHAT DO YOU THINK?"

"This is amazing, Granddad. But I don't know if any of these jobs sound exactly right for me."

"WHY NOT?"

"Well, no offense or anything, but none of these jobs sound like that much *fun*."

Granddad's bushy eyebrows squeezed together. "FUN? FUN? IT'S A JOB. IT'S NOT SUPPOSED TO BE FUN!"

Well, Diary, one thing is for sure. If jobs aren't supposed to be fun, then choosing my Winterheart Task is turning out to be a real job.

6

Artist's Block

❄ WEDNESDAY ❄

I have tried *everything* for my *This Is Me* project.

Drawing.

Watercolor.

Shadow puppets.

Claudia says I don't need to worry

about my project looking perfect,
but the things I make don't even look
subaverage!

I even tried photography. But it's
hard to take pictures that express
myself when I can't take a picture of
anything at the palace or in the sky. And
Gusty will not sit still enough for me to
photograph him!

Diary, I have heard of "writer's block," but is there such a thing as "artist's block"?

Today after school, Claudia and I walked through the gym to see if that would help give me ideas. Kids from our class were spread out across the room, using the time to work on their projects.

Adriana was painting a big mask she had made out of papier-mâché.

Reza sat in the corner with a guitar, playing a song he wrote himself.

Olive was dancing—leaping and spinning like a leaf in the wind.

"All this is art?" I whispered to Claudia.

"Remember what Ms. Collier told us?" Claudia whispered back. "Art isn't just something you make. It's also something you do."

Everyone looked so focused and into what they were doing. I wished I could be like them.

Watching Olive twirl around so

gracefully made me wonder if I could do that too.

I pointed my toes.

And held out my arms.

I spun and—

CRASH!

I bumped right into Claudia and we both tumbled over onto each other.

(Luckily, we were right next to Owen, who is making a patchwork quilt out of old soccer jerseys, so at least we had a soft landing.)

"I think dancing might not be the best choice for me," I said, helping Claudia back to her feet.

"As your doctor, I'd have to agree!"

7

Everything Is Fine

Yesterday Mom popped into my room.

"Sweetie, are you doing okay? Still working on your art project?"

I quickly shoved all my crumpled drawings under my bed. I must have started over at least fifty times. "Yup, doing just great."

"Do you want me to help you?"

For a second I thought about telling Mom how much trouble I was having with my project. But Mom has never gone to a Groundling school. Or any kind

of regular school at all! She wouldn't know how to help me.

"No thanks, Mom," I said. "I'm almost finished with it."

"I have to work on a little rain shower in the Southern Hemisphere this afternoon. Why don't you come with me? Gusty can come too."

When I was little, I used to always go with Mom to work. Since I started school at Hilltop Academy, I haven't had time for it. Maybe going with her would give me an idea for my project. Or help me choose my Task.

One thing was for sure, Diary. Nothing I did could make anything worse!

8

Mom Magic

Mom used her powers to call up a big gust of wind that zipped us through the air. Diary, I had forgotten how much fun we have soaring through the sky together!

We crossed the equator into the Southern Hemisphere, and suddenly the seasons switched. (It's autumn where we live in the north, but south of the equator it's spring. Isn't that so cool?)

Mom "parked" Gusty and me on a soft tuft of cloud. "Stay right there," she told us.

I gave her a thumbs-up. (But really, Diary, where could we go except down?)

I sat on the cloud tuft with Gusty in my lap. We shared some dried mango snacks and got ready for one of my favorite things: watching Mom work.

Mom's job is really important. She brings the gentle spring rains that help plants grow all season long.

Why the spring rains are so important:

* They help plants flower and form seeds.

* They refill streams, rivers, and lakes.

* They help crops grow that humans will harvest later.

Mom swept her hands through the air to form rain clouds. Her clouds aren't the thundering towers that Granddad makes. Mom's clouds are gentle, low, and gray.

Next, Mom leaped from cloud to cloud. Each time she landed on her tiptoes, the cloud released a little fall of rain.

She twirled and the air blew in a gentle breeze.

She moved her fingers so gracefully, opening the clouds just enough for little beams of sunlight to peek through. The raindrops scattered the sunbeams, separating the light into different colors.

A rainbow!

Mom looked back at me and winked.
I smiled. I knew she made that rainbow
just for me.

Mom's Task seems perfect for her.
I wish I could choose a Task that was
perfect for me.

Watching her, I felt so peaceful and

happy. If art is supposed to make you feel something, then Mom is definitely an artist—an artist of weather magic.

Oh my glorious sunsets, Diary—I think I just got the best idea of my entire life!

9

The Cold and the Beautiful

✳ SATURDAY ✳

I don't know why I didn't think of this sooner, Diary.

My art project should be . . . an ice sculpture!

Yes, I know. I'm never supposed to

use my winter magic at school. But nobody said anything about using my winter magic up in the clouds and then bringing my project down to the ground!

I stood in front of the mirror in my bathroom. This project is supposed to be my personal artistic expression. Well, what's more personal than my own face?

I took a deep breath. I waved my fingers very slowly around my head. Tiny ice crystals began to swirl in the bathroom. I held very still. The ice crystals began molding to my face. I usually don't mind the cold, but this was freezing!

I waited until I knew the ice had set. Then I stepped back.

Voilà! My personal portrait formed in ice! It was absolutely, icily perfect.

And yet I had this funny feeling in my stomach about it. One of Ms. Collier's rules was that we were supposed to do our projects without any help. But she didn't say anything about not using magic, right?

Right. It was fine. Totally cool. Besides, I was running out of time to think of anything else!

All I had to do next was stick the ice sculpture in the royal freezer and keep it cold until I had to take it to school.

Easy as ice cream pie.

"Lina! Come downstairs, sweetie," called Mom. "It's time to go to your grandfather's!"

Oh Diary, if only choosing my Task were this easy.

10

Choices, Choices

Today we were early for lessons with Granddad. He was still out working when we arrived at his castle.

As the North Wind, Granddad creates super-strong wind currents that circle the entire globe. This time of year he starts to get really busy because he's preparing for the winter season.

Mom, Gusty, and I stood on the balcony to watch him arrive. When a cold breeze began to blow our way, I knew he was close.

Diary, if you think Granddad can be blustery and loud on a normal day, you should see him in full Windtamer mode! He swooped across the sky with his chest puffed out and his arms spread wide. Dark gray clouds trailed behind him for miles, like a cloak.

He took a deep breath and blew it out in all directions. When the icy blast

reached me, I shivered and snuggled Gusty tightly in my arms. This was the type of wind that made you run inside for a warm blanket and a cup of hot tea. This was the wind that could change a whole season.

As cold as I was, I stayed on the balcony watching Granddad until he was finished. I felt *so* proud of him. He looked regal, commanding, and confident.

Will I ever be that sure of myself?

Once Granddad came inside (and after we all had hot tea and snowflake cookies), we got down to our lessons. To help me choose my Task, Granddad ran me through some winter magic exercises.

First I made glittering, spiky icicles.

"AH, THESE ARE GREAT, LINA. PERHAPS ICICLE-MAKING WILL BE YOUR TASK."

"Thanks, Granddad. But maybe I should do something with snow?"

I went to the courtyard and swung my arms to swirl up some thick snow clouds that dumped heaping drifts of

fluffy snow. Gusty got a big kick out
of those!

But did I really want my one Task to
be something that made people have
to shovel their sidewalks?

So we went to the pond in Granddad's
garden. I waved my hand over the

surface and froze it solid. Gusty
bounded across it and slid on his belly.

Granddad nodded at me approvingly.
"LINA: THE FREEZER OF PONDS. THAT
WOULD BE A WONDERFUL THING TO
ENTER INTO *THE BOOK OF SKIES.*"

But when I thought about writing
those words down in that big, important
book, it felt like so much pressure! Could

I really freeze ponds my whole life?

Granddad was beaming with pride.
"NEXT SATURDAY IS THE CHOOSING CEREMONY. EVERYONE WILL BE VERY EXCITED TO SEE WHAT YOU PICK."

"Hold on. What do you mean, *everyone?*"

"THE FAMILY. I'VE INVITED ALL YOUR AUNTS, UNCLES, AND COUSINS TO COME AND SHARE IN YOUR MOST SPECIAL DAY."

Gulp, Diary.

"LINA, DO YOU WANT TO CANCEL IT?" Granddad asked. **"MAYBE YOU'RE NOT READY TO CHOOSE JUST YET . . ."**

Granddad's proud look had faded. I couldn't disappoint him.

"No, no, don't cancel. I'll be ready."

The thought of my whole family watching me choose my Task made me start sweating. And that's not an easy thing to do when you're standing on a sheet of solid ice!

A High-Pressure System

This morning all the art projects were due to be turned in at school so they could be graded before the Family Showcase next week. I nearly forgot all about my ice sculpture because I had been so worried about the Choosing Ceremony and the fact that I have zero idea what I'm going to choose!

But I had to push all of that to the back of my mind because I had to focus.

I had to get an ice sculpture loaded onto a plane.

When I opened the palace freezer, my project looked just like it did when I had left it. And then that funny feeling in my stomach came back.

The sculpture was flawless—a perfect copy of my face. But I didn't feel like I had made art. I felt like I had pressed a button on a copy machine. Deep inside,

I knew this wasn't what our art project was supposed to be about.

But it was too late to change any of that now.

"Lina?" Mom called out. "Can I see?"

I threw a towel over the ice sculpture. "Um, not yet, Mom! I want it to be a surprise for the Family Showcase."

I carefully loaded the sculpture into the back of Dad's plane. I swirled a little cold air over the backseat to keep it frozen. My plan was to take it into the school, show Ms. Collier, and then stick it in the freezer in the teachers' lounge.

Easy breezy.

Dad started up the plane and off we went.

Dad is a smooth-flying pilot, but my stomach was doing barrel rolls the whole flight down to the ground. I kept thinking about the Choosing Ceremony and my Task. I also kept thinking about the Family Showcase at school. How would I explain making a perfect ice sculpture of my face without admitting that I used my winter magic to do it?

I was so nervous, Diary. My face and hands were sweaty messes.

Dad landed the plane gently in the

airfield near my school. We all got out. My parents were both sweating too. The air felt muggy and thick.

When I picked up my ice sculpture, I felt something cold hit my toe.

Drip. Drip.

With a clunk in my stomach I realized what had happened. I had been so distracted worrying about everything that I had let it get too warm in the plane.

My sculpture was melting!

Melt It All Down

I took the towel off the sculpture of my face. Except it didn't look like my face anymore at all. It was a drippy, melty blob.

Well, you can guess what happened next, Diary.

I had a total meltdown.

My eyes were dripping tears almost as fast as my ice sculpture was dripping water.

Both Mom and Dad rushed to me. "Lina, sweetheart, what's wrong?"

After a few minutes of blubbering and sobs, I managed to get out some actual words.

"My art project . . . it's . . . it's ruined!"

Mom and Dad looked at the melting ice face. They looked at my dripping real face. I braced for them to scold me, but I guess they knew I was suffering enough.

"I'm sorry . . . I know I shouldn't have used my powers to make my project . . ."

I sobbed. "I kept trying to do other
things, and it always turned out so bad.
I wanted it to look perfect, but now it
looks perfectly awful."

Dad wrapped his arms around me.
"Oh honey, no wonder you're so upset."

"It's not just that," I said, wiping a

tear from my cheek. "It's the Choosing Ceremony too. I can't think of anything I want to do for my Task. And it's so important! What if I pick the wrong thing?"

Now Mom came in for a super hug. "Lina, you don't need to choose your Task right now."

"But Granddad will be so disappointed!" I wailed.

"He'll understand," said Mom. "Besides, no matter what you choose you can always change your mind later."

I sucked a dribble of snot back into my nose. "Wait—I can?"

She smiled. "The first Task I chose for myself was Swirler of Hurricanes. I definitely didn't keep that one! I think you're putting too much pressure on yourself, Lina."

Dad put his hands on my shoulders.

"I want you to pretend that you are someone else, talking to Lina Winterheart. What would you say to yourself if you weren't you?"

I sniffled. "I don't know. That sounds kind of weird."

"Just give it a try," he said.

I took a deep breath.

And talked to myself.

A Drop in Pressure

"Lina," I said (to me). "You tried to make a perfect art project and you bombed big-time. But there's no such thing as a perfect piece of art. Anyway, this is just one project, and there will be plenty more projects to work on in the future."

I let out a big sigh and patted myself on the shoulder.

"And Lina," I said (again, to me). "You are putting too much pressure on yourself to pick your Task. It's okay if you don't know exactly what you want to do. Granddad will understand. Everyone in your family still loves you."

Talking to myself felt weird, Diary. But it also felt kind of good. It made me realize that I needed to cut myself some slack. I would never be so hard on someone else. Why should I be that hard on myself?

My parents and I hugged each other. Then we looked at the lumpy remains of my ice skull.

"Well, you could always tell your teacher it's modern art," said Dad.

That made me laugh!

"Do you want us to talk to Ms. Collier about it?" asked Mom.

"No," I said. "I'll tell her the truth. Well, not the *whole* truth. I won't tell her I used my powers to make my sculpture. But I will tell her that I couldn't finish my project in time. She may be disappointed, but I think she'll understand."

"Are you sure you're okay?" asked Mom.

I thought about it. "Yeah, I really am."

The three of us walked the rest of the way to school together. It's funny, but I actually felt like twirling. The very worst thing that could possibly happen to my art project happened, and it wasn't the end of the world. Not even close. Something about that made me feel lighter, somehow.

As we got closer to my school, the air felt lighter too. It felt still and crisp and cold.

And then something completely magical happened.

A Work of Art

Snow. The faintest, lightest dusting
of snow began falling.

The snow looked exactly how I felt on
the inside: happy and carefree.

Mom leaned down and whispered,
"Lina, are you doing this?"

"I didn't mean to," I said. "I'm sorry,

I know I'm not supposed to use my powers—"

"I thought I felt a drop in air pressure," said Dad. "That's usually what happens right before it snows."

"I think we can make an exception to the no-magic rule," said Mom. "Look."

In front of the school, kids pointed up

at the sky. Grown-ups stopped their cars
and got out to look. Everyone was smiling.

I watched them laugh as they caught
snowflakes on their tongues. I had
created something that made them happy.

It felt so good, Diary. I could do that
every day for the rest of my life.

The Task Master

Today was the Choosing Ceremony at Granddad's castle. Most of my family was there: aunts and uncles and cousins, and of course Mom and Dad and Gusty.

When Granddad called everyone into

the library and brought out *The Book of Skies*, my stomach did a nervous little flip.

I have been talking to myself more often since the day my ice sculpture melted. It doesn't feel weird anymore. It actually helps to take a step back and notice that things are hardly ever as bad as they seem.

"ARE YOU READY WITH YOUR CHOICE, LINA?"

I smiled. "Yes, Granddad, I am."

I walked up to *The Book of Skies*. I wrote my name on a fresh page, and beside it I wrote the Task I picked out for myself.

Lina Winterheart,
Maker of the First Snowfall

"LINA, I THINK THAT IS THE PERFECT TASK FOR YOU."

"Thanks, Granddad, I think so too."

(But between you and me, Diary, I wrote my choice in pencil. Just in case I change my mind.)

16

A Very Good Idea

☀ SUNDAY ☀

The Choosing Ceremony was a big
success. The best part was that
afterward, my Great-Aunt Eastia made
her famous mango-and-whipped-cloud
pudding. Talk about a work of art.

Speaking of art, I still haven't turned anything in for my *This Is Me* project. I explained to Ms. Collier that even though I didn't have anything to show her, I did learn a lot about what it means to make art.

She told me that she would give me

extra time, but I still needed to turn in a project.

I do wish I could come up with something in time for the Family Showcase tomorrow night. That snowfall I made outside the school was the perfect expression of me. If I could, I would re-create it for the Family Showcase, but I can't exactly get up onstage and make it snow!

It's too bad because I wish I could share everything I've learned over the past couple weeks. But I guess that will just have to stay as words on your pages, Diary.

Oh.

Hold on.

Words . . . pages . . .

I think I may have just had the
(actual) best idea of my entire life.

This Is Me

17

MONDAY

This evening was the Family Showcase.
The whole school was packed with
people: parents, grandparents, foster
parents, neighbors, friends. It seemed
like everyone in town came out for it!

Ms. Collier and the other teachers

had displayed the students' projects on tables in the hallways. Kids who chose to do performances were scheduled throughout the evening on the stage in the cafeteria.

Mom and Dad came with me. We watched Olive dance. We watched Reza play the guitar. Then we went out in the hall to check out more projects.

We found Claudia and her family admiring her awesome collage.

Claudia gave me a hug when she saw me. "My favorite patient!" Then she whispered, "Did Ms. Collier really let you turn your project in last minute?"

I nodded. "Come see."

I led the way to a display table down the hall. Ms. Collier stood next to it.

"Lina!" she said. "I absolutely love the project you turned in. I always knew you were creative, but I had no idea that you had such a vivid imagination!"

I blushed. "Thank you, Ms. Collier."

She stepped aside so I could show off my project. Diary, did you know that writers are artists too?

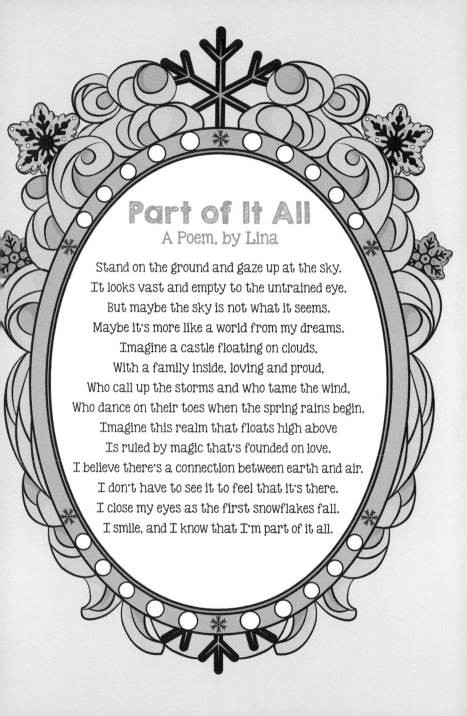

Part of It All

A Poem, by Lina

Stand on the ground and gaze up at the sky.

It looks vast and empty to the untrained eye.

But maybe the sky is not what it seems.

Maybe it's more like a world from my dreams.

Imagine a castle floating on clouds,

With a family inside, loving and proud,

Who call up the storms and who tame the wind,

Who dance on their toes when the spring rains begin.

Imagine this realm that floats high above

Is ruled by magic that's founded on love.

I believe there's a connection between earth and air.

I don't have to see it to feel that it's there.

I close my eyes as the first snowflakes fall.

I smile, and I know that I'm part of it all.

Unique As Snow

Snowflakes are some of the most beautiful examples of math in nature. You can use the power of patterns to create your own unique paper snowflakes at home!

MATERIALS:

* Paper (This is the perfect use for recycled scrap paper!) or round coffee filters
* Scissors
* Bowl or cup
* Pencil

Use a bowl to trace a circle onto a piece of paper (or use a round coffee filter). Cut out the circle. Fold the circle in half, then fold that half into thirds. You should be left with a pie-shaped piece of paper that is 1/6 of the original circle. Because of the crystal structure of ice, all snowflakes have *hexagonal*—or six-sided—symmetry.

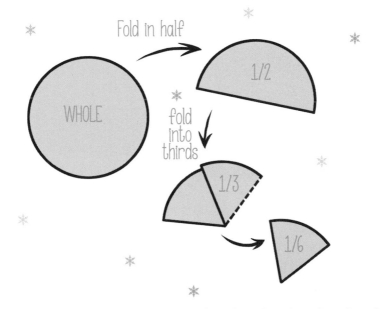

Fold in half

WHOLE

1/2

fold into thirds

1/3

1/6

Use scissors to cut patterns into your snowflake. You can't go wrong—have fun making your snowflake unique!

Experiment with how different cuts change the way your snowflake looks. What happens if you cut it like this . . .

Or like this . . .

Or like this?

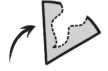

No matter how you shape the cuts, your paper snowflake will always have hexagonal symmetry—just like a real snowflake!

You can open up your snowflake after you make each cut to see how your actions affect the overall shape. With more practice, you will become better at visualizing how each cut will change the look of your snowflake. In time, you will become a master of snowflakes (just like Lina!).

Be cool—not warm—and read a sneak peek of Lina's next adventure!

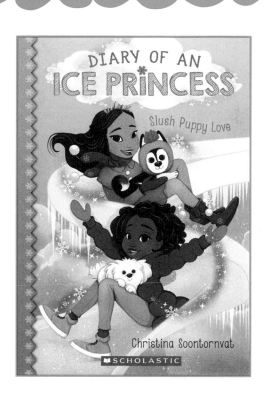

1

Beware of Brainstorms

* THURSDAY *

Dear Diary,

Today in Ms. Collier's class I learned a new word: *brainstorming*. Nope, it doesn't mean creating a storm with mind power. It means coming up with a bunch of ideas. Aren't Groundlings (also known as humans) so funny?

Our class was learning all about simple machines. Ms. Collier gave us a challenge: we had to use simple machines to move a jumbo marshmallow from one side of the classroom to the other *without* touching it at all.

If it were up to me, I would just create a blast of wintry wind to blow the marshmallow across the room—but of course I couldn't do that. My winter magic powers are a complete secret when I'm at school with Groundlings. The only person who knows about my powers is my best friend, Claudia. Luckily that's exactly who I was partnered up with.

We decided the pulley idea was the most fun. While we were sketching out our plan of action, I tried to ask Claudia some sneaky questions.

Our "Brainstorms":

* Wedge-use a ramp to get that marshmallow rolling!

* Wheel and axle-build a mini racecar for the marshmallow to ride in!

* Pulley-make a zip line and send that marshmallow soaring overhead!

"So . . ." I began. "Our family is having game night tonight. Don't you just *love* board games?"

Claudia shrugged. "Yeah, they're fun."

"Right," I said. "But not as fun as

making crafts. Don't you just *love* craft supplies?"

She looked at me funny. "Yeah, craft supplies are good . . ."

"Don't you wish you had a kit full of new craft supplies? Or beads? Don't you just *love* beads?"

Claudia put her hands on her hips. "Lina, what is all this about?"

"Your birthday is coming up and I don't know what to get you!" I blurted.

Claudia laughed. "Is that all? You know you don't have to get me anything special."

Yes, of course I know I don't *have* to. But I want to, Diary. Claudia is my best friend and she's the only person on earth (literally) who knows that I'm actually an ice princess who lives in a castle in the clouds. Plus, Claudia always gets me perfect presents. This year she got me gloves knitted with conductive thread so I can still play video games in the middle of a blizzard!

"Well, what are your parents getting you?" I asked.

"They promised me that this year I could finally get a puppy . . ."

Perfect! I'd get Claudia a collar for her new dog!

". . . but then last week we learned my dad is allergic." She sighed sadly. "The best I can hope for is a gecko."

Diary, I feel so bad for Claudia. She has always wanted a dog. Whatever present I come up with for her needs to be so good that she'll forget all about wanting a puppy.

2

Magically Miffed

✳ FRIDAY ✳

Today after school I brainstormed a list of all the things I could get Claudia for her birthday.

Possible Gifts:

✳ A stuffed toy dog.

✳ A sweatshirt with a dog on the front.

✳ A dog-of-the-month calendar.

But Claudia already has so many dog-themed things. None of those gifts seemed like something she would really want.

Then I heard Mom calling my name from downstairs. "Lina! I need you to come here right now, young lady!"

Anytime Mom calls me *young lady* I know it can't be good.

Downstairs, Mom stood in the dining room with her arms crossed. "Lina, did you leave the pitcher of lemonade out again?"

Uh-oh. I'm not supposed to leave any food or drinks out because Gusty will jump up and get into it. Sure enough, I looked down and saw him sitting in the middle of a sticky puddle with a guilty look on his face.

"Please get a towel and clean all of this up," said Mom. "And then give Gusty a bath."

"Okay, I will," I said.

As soon as Mom walked out of the room, Gusty started whining.

"Don't give me that look," I said. "This is all your fault. Lucky for you, I can get this cleaned up in a jiffy."

I pushed up my sleeves and held out my hands. I blew a cold breath over my fingers and pointed them at the puddle of lemonade. The sticky liquid froze into icy crystals that rose up off the floor and swirled into a frosty cloud. A lemonade cloud!

I waved my hands and sent the lemonade cloud flying out the dining room door to the courtyard.

"Easy, freezy," I said with a smile. "Now, Gusty, let's get you into the bath."

A few minutes later, Gusty was enjoying his soapy bath upstairs when I heard Mom yelling again.

"LINA WINDTAMER RUDDER WINTERHEART, GET DOWN HERE RIGHT NOW, YOUNG LADY!"

Ooh, when Mom calls me young lady

and uses my full name, I know I'm in gigantic trouble.

I grabbed a soaking wet Gusty and ran down to Mom's office. The lemonade cloud hovered over her desk and was raining sticky drops all over her papers! I must have sent the cloud out the wrong door!

"Lina, I told you to clean up that mess!"

"I did! I cleaned it up with magic."

"Lina, not every problem should be solved with magic. Your powers are getting stronger and you need to think before you use them. You will clean this up. *With a towel this time.*"

Diary, do you know what *miffed* means? It means mad, but not super mad. Like halfway between mad and annoyed.

As I sopped up the lemonade with the towel, I was miffed at Mom. For months my family has been pushing me to get better at using my magic powers. Well, I got better! And now she wants me to stop?

Good thing tomorrow is Saturday. On Saturdays I go to Granddad's castle.

"Granddad will understand," I grumbled.

Talk about words I never thought I'd say!

Now check out Lina's first adventure!

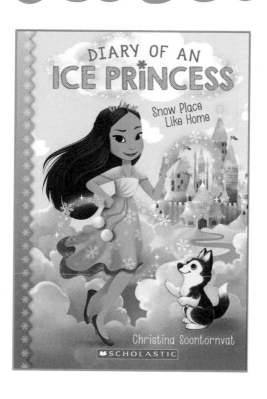

THE NIGHT BEFORE THE BIG DAY

* FRIDAY *

Tonight is the perfect night to start a new diary because there is no way I can fall asleep!

Tomorrow is our family picnic. Why am I so excited, Diary? It's just a normal, old family picnic, right?

Except our picnic is in the clouds.

And our family is definitely *not* normal.

I just triple-checked all my stuff for tomorrow:

Lucky socks ✔

Lucky purple tiara ✔

Lucky dress (the only one I have that isn't ripped!) ✔

(Okay, there is a tiny rip at the shoulder and a stain on the front, but that's it!)

Normally I wouldn't be allowed to go out dressed like this. After all, I'm a princess. But Mom and Dad didn't say anything about it. I guess they know I need all the luck I can get tomorrow.

When they tucked me in tonight, they gave me a pep talk.

"Everything is going to be fine, Lina," said Dad.

"When it's time, just relax, breathe, and let the wind take you," Mom reminded me.

My mom is a Windtamer. All Windtamers have the power to control the wind and weather. Whenever she wants to go somewhere, she just waves her hand and calls up a gust of wind. The wind holds her up and carries her wherever she tells it to go.

CHRISTINA SOONTORNVAT grew up behind the counter of her parents' Thai restaurant, reading stories. These days she loves to make up her own, especially if they involve magic. Christina also loves science and worked in a science museum for years before pursuing her dream of being an author. She still enjoys cooking up science experiments at home with her two young daughters. You can learn more about Christina and her books on her website at soontornvat.com.

JOIN THE ROYAL MERMAID RESCUE CREW!

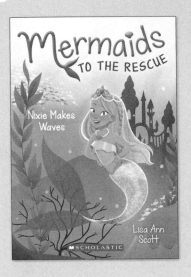

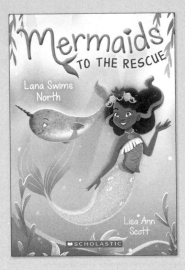

Be brave and keep the seas safe.

Princess Tabby is no scaredy-cat!

Oh my glaciers, Diary!

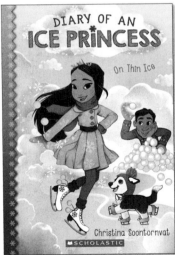

Princess Lina is the *coolest* girl in school!